Happy Thanksgiving Rebus

By David A. Adler

Illustrated by Jan Palmer

Viking

VIKING
Published by the Penguin Group
Viking Penguin, a division of Penguin Books USA Inc.,
375 Hudson Street, New York, New York 10014, U.S.A.
Penguin Books Ltd, 27 Wrights Lane, London W8 5TZ, England
Penguin Books Australia Ltd, Ringwood, Victoria, Australia
Penguin Books Canada Ltd, 2801 John Street, Markham, Ontario, Canada L3R 1B4
Penguin Books (N.Z.) Ltd, 182–190 Wairau Road, Auckland 10, New Zealand
Penguin Books Ltd, Registered Offices: Harmondsworth, Middlesex, England
First published in 1991 by Viking Penguin, a division of Penguin Books USA Inc.

1   3   5   7   9   10   8   6   4   2

Text copyright © David A. Adler
Illustrations copyright © Jan Palmer
All rights reserved

Library of Congress Catalog Card Number: 91-50267
ISBN 0-670-83388-6

Printed in the U.S.A.
Set in 14 point Bookman

In *Happy Thanksgiving Rebus,* many words or parts of words are replaced with pictures. A word written with a picture or pictures is called a rebus.

Some of the rebuses are easy to read. is bread. is turkey. Other rebuses are more difficult. is tiny. S𝖳 is stack.

If you have trouble reading some of the rebuses, check the glossary on page 30. The same story without rebuses begins on page 24. Have fun!

CHAPTER 1
Two Pieces of Cake

It was the morning of Thanksgiving Day. J☀ was

helping his 🍐ents pre🍐 the holiday dinner.

1st they made the stuffing from 🍞 , 🧅 , 🥬 ,

🌿 , & 🧴 . J☀ helped clean & stuff the 🍗 .

Then J☀'s mother put the 🦃 in 2 the 📺

2 cook.

J mixed • sauce with , , & .

He helped his father wash the vege & make

the .

"Now we the ," J 's father said.

It was a big . J imagined the large piece

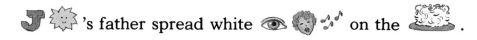

his mother give him. He might even ask 4 a

2ND piece of & eat that, 2.

J 's father spread white on the .

He made & from

& put them on . J knew that his father &

mother did like 2 eat the decorations from the

of a , so he eat them all.

"Now let's set the [table]," his father said.

J[sun]'s [p]ents took a large S[T] of [beans] from the [boat][tree].

"[Y] do we [r][D] so [people][E] [beans]?" J[sun] asked.

"[ant][rose] is coming [4] dinner," J[sun]'s mother said.

J[sun] remembered that [ant][rose] liked [2] have some [T] & a piece of [cake] [4] dessert.

May[bee] there will [pretzel] [bee] enough [4] me [2] have a [2ND] piece of [cake], J[sun] thought, but still, [eye] will eat the decorations off the [top] of the [cake].

J 's father said, " & Cousins & R coming 4 dinner with their children, , KT, & ry."

J remembered that Cousin L loved .

, KT, & ry loved , 2 .

& J have 2 share the decorations with , KT, & ry.

14

"Our friends **LN & JR** coming **2**," **J**'s

mother said.

"**Y** must they all come?" **J** asked. "👁 may

🥨 get **NE** 🎂 at all."

"They **R** coming 🐝cause we invited them,"

J's mother said. "We like **2** share what we have

with our family **&** friends."

CHAPTER 2

The Pilgrims

J☀ went 2 his room. A little Y le later, his mother

stood by the 🚪. "May 👁 come in?" she asked.

"Yes, Mommy."

J☀'s mother sat on the 🛏 & said, "Let me

tell U about Thanksgiving.

"👥E y 👂👂 ago the 🧑‍🦱👩 left England & came

2 the New World, 2 America. They came on a ⛵

named the May🌼. They landed on Plymouth 🪨, in

Massachusetts, in 1620.

"They had a terrible winter. 👥E died. In the Ɛ,

& 🪗 & where **2** hunt & 🐟 . That fall, the 👒👒 had a good har 🟫 . They had plen **T** of food **4** the coming winter. They celebrated with a **3** day feast."

"What did the 👒👒 eat at the par **T**, Mommy?"

"They **8** 🦆🦆 , 🦢 , wild 🦃 & 🦌 , 🫘 , 🍓 , 🎃 , & 🌽 . 🧍🧍 E 👤👤 joined them. The 👒👒 were thankful **2** 🐝

18

2gether with family **&** friends **&** **2** have enough **2** share with them. We're thankful, **2**. We have plen**T** **2** eat **&** we're happy **2** share what we have with our family **&** friends."

J☀ was happy **2** share the 🦃 , stuffing, • sauce, and 🥗. But he wished he could have more than **1** piece of 🥧 **4** dessert.

CHAPTER 3

The Guests Arrive

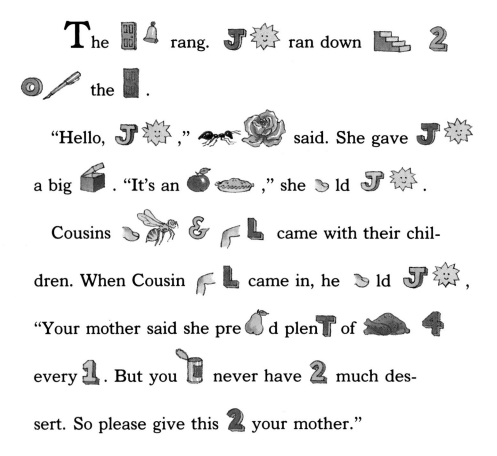

The rang. ran down 2 the .

"Hello, ," said. She gave a big . "It's an ," she ld .

Cousins & came with their children. When Cousin came in, he ld , "Your mother said she pre d plenT of 4 every 1. But you never have 2 much dessert. So please give this 2 your mother."

He gave J☀ 2 📦📦 🪱d 2gether with a 🐛. "It's a 🎃 🥧 & some 🍪," Cousin ⌐L said.

LN & J brought 🌸🌸 4 J☀'s 🍐ents & 🥫D 4 J☀.

J☀ talked & played with ⬭, KT, & 🐔ry. Then, when every 1 was about 2 eat, J☀'s father whispered 2 him, "Now we have 🍰, 🥧, 🍪 , & 🥫D. U will have a lot more dessert than just 1 piece of 🍰."

" 🐜🌹, Cousins 🐝 & ⌐L, ⬭, KT, 🐔ry, LN, & J R just like me," J☀ 🍂ld his father. "They like 2 share, 2."

THE STORY
WITHOUT
REBUSES

CHAPTER 1
Two Pieces of Cake

It was the morning of Thanksgiving Day. Jason was helping his parents prepare the holiday dinner.

First they made the stuffing from bread, onions, celery, parsley, and oil. Jason helped clean and stuff the turkey. Then Jason's mother put the turkey into the oven to cook.

Jason mixed cranberry sauce with pineapple, nuts, and raisins. He helped his father wash the vegetables and make the salad.

"Now we can ice the cake," Jason's father said.

It was a big cake. Jason imagined the large piece his mother would give him. He might even ask for a second piece of cake and eat that, too.

Jason's father spread white icing on the cake. He made tiny pumpkins and flowers from orange icing and put them on top. Jason knew that his father and mother did not like to eat the decorations from the top of a cake, so he would eat them all.

"Now let's set the table," his father said.

Jason's parents took a large stack of dishes from the pantry.

"Why do we need so many dishes?" Jason asked.

"Aunt Rose is coming for dinner," Jason's mother said.

Jason remembered that Aunt Rose liked to have some tea and a piece of cake for dessert.

Maybe there will not be enough for me to have a second piece of cake, Jason thought, but still, I will eat the decorations off the top of the cake.

Jason's father said, "And Cousins Toby and Neil are coming for dinner with their children, Penny, Katie, and Henry."

Jason remembered that Cousin Neil loved cake. Penny, Katie, and Henry loved cake, too. And Jason would have to share the cake decorations with Penny, Katie, and Henry.

"Our friends Ellen and Jay are coming too," Jason's mother said.

"Why must they all come?" Jason asked. "I may not get any cake at all."

"They are coming because we invited them," Jason's mother said. "We like to share what we have with our family and friends."

CHAPTER 2
The Pilgrims

Jason went to his room. A little while later, his mother stood by the door. "May I come in?" she asked.

"Yes, Mommy."

Jason's mother sat on the bed and said, "Let me tell you about Thanksgiving.

"Many years ago the Pilgrims left England and came to the New World, to America. They came on a ship named the *Mayflower*. They landed on Plymouth Rock, in Massachusetts, in 1620.

"They had a terrible winter. Many died. In the spring, Indians taught the Pilgrims how to plant corn, beans, and squash and where to hunt and fish. That fall, the Pilgrims had a good harvest. They had plenty of food for the coming winter. They celebrated with a three day feast."

"What did the Pilgrims eat at the party, Mommy?"

"They ate ducks, geese, wild turkey and deer, nuts, berries, pumpkins, and corn. Many Indians joined them. The

Pilgrims were thankful to be together with family and friends and to have enough to share with them. We're thankful, too. We have plenty to eat and we're happy to share what we have with our family and friends."

Jason was happy to share the turkey, stuffing, cranberry sauce, and salad. But he wished he could have more than one piece of cake for dessert.

CHAPTER 3
The Guests Arrive

The doorbell rang. Jason ran downstairs to open the door.

"Hello, Jason," Aunt Rose said. She gave Jason a big box. "It's an apple pie," she told Jason.

Cousins Toby and Neil came with their children. When Cousin Neil came in, he told Jason, "Your mother said she prepared plenty of turkey for everyone. But you can never have too much dessert. So please give this to your mother."

He gave Jason two boxes tied together with a ribbon. "It's a pumpkin pie and some cookies," Cousin Neil said.

Ellen and Jay brought flowers for Jason's parents and candy for Jason.

Jason talked and played with Penny, Katie, and Henry. Then, when everyone was about to eat, Jason's father whispered to him, "Now we have cake, pie, cookies, and candy. You will have a lot more dessert than just one piece of cake."

"Aunt Rose, Cousins Toby and Neil, Penny, Katie, Henry, Ellen, and Jay are just like me," Jason told his father. "They like to share, too."

GLOSSARY

The rebuses in this glossary are in the
order they first appear in the story.

 Jason		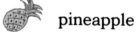 to, too, two
ents parents		• cranberry
pre prepare		pineapple
1ST first		nuts
bread		raisins
onions		vege vegetables
celery		salad
parsley		can
& and		ice
oil		cake
turkey		would
in 2 into		4 for
oven		2ND second

 icing

tiny

pumpkins

flowers

orange

top

not

table

S T stack

dishes

pantry

Y why

need

many

aunt

Rose

T tea

may maybe

be

I

Toby

L Neil

R are

Penny

K T Katie

ry Henry

L N Ellen

J Jay

N E any

cause because

Y le while

door

bed

U you

y years

Pilgrims

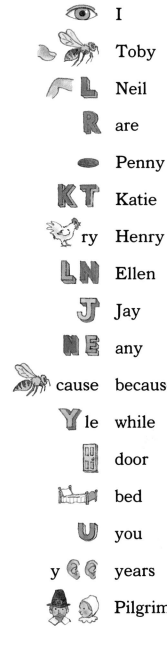

 ship

May *Mayflower*

 Rock

 spring

 Indians

 plant

 corn

 beans

 squash

 fish

har harvest

plen plenty

 three

par  party

 ate

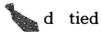 ducks

 geese

 deer

 berries

 gether together

 one

 doorbell

 stairs

 open

 box

 apple

 pie

 ld told

every  everyone

 d tied

ribbon

cookies

candy